The Decision Maker
Power, Pride, and Paper

By Rex Voge

Dorrance Publishing Co
585 Alpha Drive
Pittsburgh, PA 15238
Visit our website at www.dorrancebookstore.com

ISBN: 979-8-8860-4108-8
eISBN: 979-8-8860-4775-2

Chapter 1

A chair slides out from under a table. A weathered detective sits down.

A tape recorder clicks on.

"This is Detective Aaron Phillips, interview with Thomas Marcini October 6, 1989." The detective looks across the table at a well-groomed, thin-looking man nearly 30 years old.

"So, you came here, means you have something worth telling me."

"That's right, detective, starts back in nineteen-twenty-two."

"The story I hear only starts two weeks ago. Just tell me about the judge."

"No, no, detective. You don't JUST wanna hear about the judge, you wanna hear the story from the beginning. So go get some coffee, pull up a chair, and get cozy. you're in for a ride." Marcini smiles.

"Nineteen-twenty-two my grandfather Vincenzo, the strong Italian with pure ideals, and a man who wanted to stamp his name on the world immigrated from Napoli and immediately moved into Brooklyn. He was twenty years old. Shortly after his move, he went to work for a man named Arthur Cantrell, a tall, well-built, German man, whose family made a fortune on liquor over the last sixty years. With the prohibition in full swing, Cantrell needed people who wanted to work, wanted to get paid, and didn't need too many details.

"My grandfather was the perfect man for the job. Having just arrived in the United States, Grandpa could slide under anyone's radar. If he looked lost, it's probably because he was. So when Cantrell needed a driver to deliver some hooch, there was Grandpa. Now Arthur ran New York's underground booze. If you were stilling, moving, or selling, you knew Arthur by name. Now my grandfather started as a runner, if you needed liquor across town, he would hop in that sweet model-A, and run it anywhere."

"How did your grandfather avoid getting caught? I mean, the bootlegging cops were all over New York."

"Oh yeah, they were. But Grandad knew how to sneak by 'em. He could dress that model-A a million ways and never draw suspicion. It also helped that being new to New York he could ask anyone even police officers for directions and because most people are polite, they'd help. Pretty soon though, he worked his way into being a connections man. He could make friends anywhere. And he did.

"He made friends from Long Island to Queens and everywhere in between. For eight years, my grandfather made Mr. Cantrell richer than the President, and in the process made a lot of connections of his own. Then Nineteen Thirty happened, the prohibition gets worse, and then the Depression hits. Less booze flowing, less money, and more problems."

"Yeah, I suppose trying to push alcohol around the city got difficult. Can't be mad though, you had to expect it, right?" detective Phillips sneered.

"Oh no, moving it wasn't the problem," Marcini replies. "Storing it was. They were making more booze than they had room for. The way Grandpa tells it, you couldn't move six feet in the warehouse without bumping into product. Then when they handed prohibition law to the judicial system, it got worse. Cops like you didn't even need probable cause to search places like warehouses or dockyards. They could walk in, cuff ya, and take all your liquor. They called it, 'protecting the peace of the city.' Then they'd turn around and sell it to the bars that would pay the most for it. Talk about protect and serve.

"But I have to say, thank God for the winter of thirty-three. The pinheads that called themselves our leaders finally got wise and repealed that stupid amendment. I think either they realized they can't stop people from boozing, or they crunched the numbers and discovered they could make bank on legal booze. It went from good to great when the war started, they started using Uncle Sam's boys to move liquor, and sales went through the roof.

"Twenty bucks a bottle got a soldier everything he needed to make the long boat ride over to France. During the war, Grandad managed to keep his contacts happy, and in return, they made sure to give him their exclusive business and Grandpa made a lot of cash. When victory in Germany was announced, you woulda thought it was New Year's. Everybody bought our booze and partied in the streets. It was like a weight was lifted off the world, and everybody took a deep breath. Grandpa though, he made a lot of money."

Chapter 2

Thomas Marcini holds a picture of Arthur Cantrell, who is posing next to a whiskey cask.

"January second, nineteen-fifty-one. My grandfather walked into Cantrell's office and handed him a check for one-hundred-thousand dollars. Looked him in the eye and said, 'This means I no longer work for you. I've paid my debt, I'm glad we've had our time together, but the time has come for me to spread my wings.'

"Then he went into business for himself. By nineteen-fifty, my grandfather was married and had three sons, my father Michael, my Uncle Diego, the one who ran my grandfather's books, and my Uncle Lucio, the one who monitored security. Then he performed a miracle and convinced his four brothers to move to his house in Brooklyn. Try telling four full-blooded Italians that America is the place to be when they can get the best food from right down the street.

"But Grandad did it. His brothers pulled their roots in Napoli and moved to Grandpa's house in Bensonhurst. Grandad figured out how to get business going and put his brothers to work. All he had to do was build a network. As I said, my grandfather could make friends anywhere, and he had connections from Baltimore to Boston. Grandpa was into all of it, he had one brother in charge of stolen cars, one in charge of bootlegging, one for loans and collections, and one to run nightclubs around the city. And before anyone knew it, we were the largest organization on the east coast. We were slowly growing into Brooklyn, and no one was getting wise. Hell, we practically set up a money-laundering scheme right down the street from the police. Not for bragging, but the location was just prime. Pop open a new laundromat here, maybe a dry cleaner. Then wait a couple of months, and open a bar.

"How did you avoid collapsing? Phillips asks. I mean you, couldn't keep the whole business in the family, right? You needed help. How'd you pull that off?"

"You're right, detective. We needed outside help. But you can't just take any meathead and make him a leader, you need guys that work hard, fight hard, and don't talk. And that's exactly what we got. When my grandpa brought Stone in, he asked him to train our boys to fight. Not just throw hands and pull triggers, he needed hard soldiers who wouldn't ask too many questions. After that, we needed to get our chop shops going, and for that we needed mechanics. So, Stone did what he needed to do. Find wrench turners that wanted to make a lot of dough, and he hired the ones that did the best. And damn, were they good.

"They could take any car from the street, clean it, clone it, and sell it out of state at a markup and no one ever caught on, and pretty soon money was rolling in. Then there was a storage problem. So much cash was coming in so fast, that we didn't have anywhere to put it. I mean, we couldn't just stack it up at home and pray nobody started asking questions, and with that, we found our solution. We bought banks around the city so we could store our cash and leave the authorities to their imagination.

"We managed to stay clear of trouble through the sixties, even when the cops were slamming down hard on organized crime. My father Michael worked for my great Uncle Anthony in the loans and collections department. He would go to the Village Gate, where he met the collectors for a 'business meeting' and they would talk about who they collected from, how much, and who got an extension. My father took detailed notes and took in all the cash, then he would give it to his uncle, who recorded it and gave it to my Uncle Diego. He would take those records and give my grandfather a monthly update."

"So that's how it works," Detective Phillips smirks. "The collectors stay clean because it just looks like regular business, and the boss never has to show his face."

"That's right," Marcini smiles. "It's easy when all you have to do is walk in the club and grab a table in the back. The only people who care are the wait staff."

Chapter 3

"I was born in nineteen-sixty, and I never met him until I was ten."

"So, he worked for your grandfather for eleven years before you even saw his face?"

"That's right, detective, he was the kind of guy who didn't come around until he needed to. He usually worked over the phone. Someone had a problem, call Eli, tell him what you know, and he'll handle it."

July 18, 1971. Vincenzo Marcini sits at the desk in his office talking to his brother Anthony, a tall well-aged man in his fifties, his son Michael, a heavyset man with thick round glasses and short, parted brown hair, and two of Michael's collectors known as "Tyson" and "Ross."

"Dad, we have a problem. Tyson tells me they just come from Remano's Little Italy, and Martin refuses to pay on his loan."

"Is this true, Tyson?" Vincenzo asks, peering over his glasses.

"Yes sir, Mr. Marcini," Tyson whines. "We went to collect this week's payment and he told us, 'Go to hell, you thieving Bastardos.'"

"That's right, Mr. Marcini," Ross spits. "He told us he's not paying anymore and there's nothing we can do about it. He said, 'Go back to your throne and forget about it.'"

Vincenzo taps his fingers on his desk.

"Please leave. I need to make a phone call.

Thomas Marcini.

"Now they all knew who he was calling, but because they respected the relationship between him and Grandad, they all left the room."

Marcini flips through photographs.

"Ah, I always loved that car. A nineteen-fifty-seven Plymouth Fury, four hundred ponies in the rear wheels, and he had her custom painted. She was deep purple with gold stripes going from the headlights to the end of the tail fins. It was the one thing he cared about the most, and nobody ever gave him grief about the color. I remember my father did once," he says.

"Purple is for girls, is that what you want to be when you grow up? A girl?"

"He stood up from the dinner table, picked up my father's chair with my father still in it, and threw him out the picture window in the dining room. Dad fell fifteen feet and broke his right arm and leg. He sat up, looked at my grandfather, and said, 'Are you going to do something about that?'"

"My grandfather said, 'Who made fun of the car? Me or you?'"

"We all sat back down and finished our dinner before we took dad to the hospital."

"I guess when you love something that much, you tend to take things personally," Detective Phillips grins.

"Yeah, we thought the same thing. "

Chapter 4

"Eli Stone. Whenever you saw that car, you knew a decision was about to be made. Sometimes it was a good thing, sometimes it was a very, very bad thing. Bad if you had disrespected my grandfather or anyone in the family for that matter. It was always fun hearing the stories people would tell some days after Eli would come down. 'It looked like a lightning bolt coming down the road.' 'He yelled so loud that the plaster in my living room cracked.' That one made me laugh the hardest. All it meant is that he took his job seriously and with pride.

"Stone's job was to protect the business in every aspect of what we did. When we had a serious problem that needed solving now, we called him. And based on his knowledge of the situation, he would make his decision. A lot of the time, he just dealt with people who didn't want to pay their loans anymore, but sometimes it was somebody in our organization who was milking our payroll a little too much and needed to be 'fired.' That was a task he enjoyed the least. One of the people he hired and trained wanted to steal some extra green, and he had to put a stop to it. Nonetheless, he was good at his job, and we loved him for it.

"No one ever tried to tell him he was wrong. His decision was the last word and God forbid you do not follow his instructions; you should have packed before you made bad choices. Because he came down on you like the Holy Ghost."

"If his word was last, why did everyone love him the way they did?"

"Because detective, his decisions made sure everyone involved would benefit. Sometimes, that meant an entire neighborhood received an envelope full of cash.

"Like the time 'Champagne' Teddy Montaigne refused to pay my grandfather for the protection service he provided. We sent the manpower to make sure his deal went easy, and in return, we'd get twenty percent of the deal. So when Teddy chose not to pay, Eli was sent to change his mind. Stone decided to buy Teddy's neighborhood instead. He collected our twenty and gave it to the people in Lefferts Gardens, the neighborhood that Montaigne ran. He promised to give them all of Teddy's money if they helped him push Teddy out. Three months later, Mr. Champagne himself came to my grandfather for a loan. That's why they loved him. He was one of the good guys, and even the ones who stood against him had respect.

"I'll never forget the night my grandfather asked him to talk to Remano about his loan. It was like hearing that famous quote. 'Down goes Frasier!'

A purple 1957 Plymouth Fury parks in front of Remano's Little Italy. A coarse, long-bearded man with freshly cut short hair steps out. He wears worn brown leather steel toe boots, tan canvas pants, and an olive-brown button-down jacket. He closes the car door and walks into the restaurant to speak with the hostess.

"I'm looking for Martin."

"He's in his office. I'll go get him."

"No. Take me to him. I need to speak to him now."

"Yes sir, of course right this way, um, follow me."

The hostess leads the stranger to meet Mr. Remano, a short, cultured, Italian man with curly black hair, steel-framed glasses, and a bruise on his right cheek.

"M-Mr. Remano, this man says he needs to talk to you, and uh, he can't wait."

"It's okay, Susie, let him in."

"I'm Eli Stone, here to talk about your loan with Mr. Marcini."

"I know who you are, you are the ghoul he sends to make sure I comply with his demands," Remano snarls. "I know how his loan works, I knew what I was getting into, yes, I agreed to pay weekly. I also agreed to pay his price per week. But I did not agree to take a beating to remind me to pay. How am I supposed to make money if I have no customers? I have no customers because they do not want to look at a man with a broken face. Now I am losing money and have nothing but bruises to show for it."

"Beatings, who is beating you?"

"Your men, they call themselves Tyson and Ross. They hurt my hand today because I do not have one thousand dollars for my loan payment."

Stone takes Remano's hand into his.

"Tyson and Ross did this?"

"They are the men who come to me for payment. When I started coming up short, they started hurting me to remind me the punishment for making them come back during the week."

"I see. Can I use your phone? I need to make a call."

"Sure."

"Hello, Mr. Marcini? Question, are Tyson and Ross still at the house? They are good, put Tyson on the phone, please? Thanks. Tyson? Stone. I need you to come over to Remano's right away. On your way here, stop at the drug store and pick up a right-hand wrist brace. That's right, a right-hand wrist brace. Okay, see you soon."

"What are you going to do, Mr. Stone?" Remano asks.

"Hurting people is not our way of doing business. I am going to make sure it never happens again."

"Okay."

"We'll wait outside for my friends."

"Okay, Mr. Stone."

Twenty minutes later, a yellow Mercury Comet parks in front of Remano's Little Italy.

"Here's the brace you asked for, Stone, why need it anyway?" Tyson shouts.

Eli Stone starts a fistfight. A flurry of punches, kicks, and a headbutt, amidst a whirlwind of foul language, the likes of which have never been seen before. In the process, Tyson's nose and jaw are broken, and Ross is thrown headfirst into the passenger door.

"WHO GAVE YOU PERMISSION TO HURT PEOPLE WHO OWE US MONEY? Did you think I wouldn't find out?"

"No! We wanted to send a message that we get paid no matter what," Tyson whimpers.

"A message is marking his calendar in bright red ink! People who can't use their hands can't give us what we're owed! This is what's going to happen, Mr. Remano, you were paying one thousand dollars per week. Now you pay two hundred fifty dollars per week. Also, you will no longer build interest on your loan and the interest already built is paid. That said, you owe us a total of sixteen thousand dollars. And with it, you have room to breathe. Do you agree to these conditions?"

"Yes, Mr. Stone, I do."

"Then, sign your name here. Now, your wrist is broken. So I want you to wear this brace on your hand every day for the next five weeks. Can you do that?"

"Happily, Mr. Stone."

"Good. Go inside and enjoy your evening. And if I ever hear that you two hurt anyone else, there won't be a hole deep enough for me to bury you. Understood?"

"Yes sir."

Remano goes back inside his restaurant as Stone rummages through Tyson and Ross's belongings. Satisfied, Stone gets into his car and drives to the Marcini house, goes inside, and sits down for dinner.

Vincenzo sits down at the table and looks over at Eli.

"Did you work things out with Remano?"

"I did."

Stone passes a folded sheet of paper down the table and watches Vincenzo read.

"You made a new agreement with Martin?" Vincenzo questions.

"Had to. Tyson and Ross were beating him for cash, and he was tapped out."

"Looking at your hands, I'd say you retrained them in collecting from debtors?"

"Just enough to make them think twice about doing it again. They're on their way to get fixed up."

"I see you also stopped all interest and forgave the interest already on the account."

"Man pays his loan better when he knows he's only paying principal. Besides, we have three more cars lined up and those sales alone will make up for the lost interest."

"True, but I can't overlook two thousand in previous interest."

Eli throws two cash-filled wallets on the table.

"Tyson and Ross shared your opinion and decided to square it up."

"You can be convincing, I'll give you that. You are convincing." Vincenzo smiles.

Detective Phillips leans in.

"All those years Stone worked for your family, and your grandfather never wanted him dead. Why? I mean he did come from another crime faction."

"That's true, detective, but my grandfather knew all about him. Eli was drafted into Korea when he was twenty-one, and he was assigned to a recon unit. Those guys saw the worst in humanity. He never told any stories, but we knew he was haunted by the things he'd seen. After his discharge, he went to work as a 'problem solver' for a Russian mob led by Josef Urokov.

"A mean drunk who led his organization from his ball sack. The guy had no brains. When he felt slighted by a competitor, he just had him killed. That was a bad time to be from Yonkers. Urokov hated the competition that came outta there, so it was a shock when he started getting pressure from my grandfather. Josef thought he ruled Brooklyn, and when he started getting squeezed out by my grandfather's business, he sent Stone to kill him. So, like a good soldier, he went out to find the best place to do the job. Three days into his search, he learned just how good and kind my grandfather is to the people who work for him. Not that my grandpa was soft, but that he knew when it was time for discipline, and when it was time for compassion. That's what I think changed Eli's heart. He saw kindness in an otherwise dark world.

"So, he made a different choice. Eli went back to the nightclub owned by Urokov, walked right into his office while he was in a meeting with his top guys discussing how to push us out of New York. Stone pulls his pistol and shoots Josef three times right in the forehead. He looks at the other men in the room, holsters his gun, and says, 'You can leave now.' And he just turns around and walks out. The next day, he walks into my grandfather's office in the warehouse he bought, lays down the day's paper, and says, 'I used to work for him, he wanted you dead. Now I'm looking for work.' And my grandfather says. 'Well, I suppose I could use a man like you.' And the rest, as they say, detective, is history."

Chapter 5

Detective Phillips pulls out a strip of newspaper that reads, "Mob war erupts in Brooklyn, twenty-eight dead."

"So, you seem to know something about this. Care to share?"

"Oh man, that was a rough time. The whole year of seventy-three was a bad time to be in our line of work, Cesar de Santa was quickly takin' over Queens and we were just on the other side. So when he started feeling pressure from our side of Irving Avenue, he told his people to target our people. They killed seven guys in one of our chop shops and ripped off a lot of our products. So, my grandfather sent Eli to investigate. The minute he rolled into Queens tracking a lead, he was surrounded by Cesar's' gunmen, they tried hosing him down with lead, but they didn't know who they were dealin' with. One of them got lucky and sent a bullet through his shoulder, and he had to race out of there and get to the hospital A.S.A.P.

"He spent seven weeks in the hospital getting stronger, and angrier. He learned from my uncle Lucio that de Santa had ordered the hit on our chop shop, and he spent the rest of his time recovering, and planning. How he'd get de Santa, and how he'd make him pay. I tell you, man, I've never seen someone go from calm to rage then back to calm in less than a minute before, and I never wanna see it again. Like how a hurricane disappears right before it falls on Miami. He was seething when Uncle Lucio gave him the news, and then he went silent and just said. 'Thank you,' and went back to sleep. Two weeks later he gets, released from the hospital and he comes over to the house.

"An excited Vincenzo Marcini jumps up from the dinner table as Eli Stone approaches the front door. He has planned a grand welcome for the man he calls a son. Fresh veal, alfredo as far as the eye can see, and wine straight from the motherland.

"'Mio Amico! My friend! Brother, how are you? You look like a man with a heavy mind, you haven't been sweating our problem in Queens, have you?"

"'I'm well, Padre, I'm getting stronger every day. I also thank God for sparing me. He should have taken me, but I am alive, and it's all that matters. As far as Cesar de Santa, I think I solved that problem. I've been talking to my spies in Queens, and they tell me that Cesar gets money from home to fund his operations. I say we find out when his money comes in, and we take it ourselves. This part is important. We need him to think that our dispute is settled. Once we start squeezing his cash flow, he'll get desperate and start asking us for help. A time will come when he can't keep asking for cash from home, he'll need to get it elsewhere. Then we can put him out of our misery. He cost us time and money. Not to mention, his idiots put a bullet in me. If we can make him want it enough, he will come crawling. That's when you do your thing to draw him in, and we bait a trap. He wants to play the mouse, and we'll let him.'

"So that's what we did." Thomas Marcini grins.

"On the third of the month, we collected a 'care package' from Rio de Janeiro. And every thirty days, we got a hundred-grand richer. And come October of seventy-three, Cesar de Santa called a 'sit down' with my grandfather. He wanted to meet in Queens, but Grandpa said, 'eh, no. If you want to meet, you'll come to Brooklyn.'

October twenty-third. Cesar de Santa has demanded a meeting between him and Vincenzo Marcini. Headlights flood an empty lot in Flatbush as de Santa approaches the meeting where Vincenzo stands in front of a large wooden crate. Eli Stone stands in the shadow just out of Cesar's' view.

"Well, you have been calling me nonstop for a week now. What do you want?

"It's simple. I need to keep my business running, and I have no more money. I want to bring you into my operation, you start funding my progress, and you get thirty percent return per month."

"You want me to settle for thirty percent!" Vincenzo laughs. Thirty percent doesn't even pay my tailor. How do you expect me to fund you and live with thirty percent?"

"It's a fair deal. You make ten times more in Brooklyn than you let on. You should take the deal."

"Did no one ever tell you never negotiate from a position of weakness? You have nothing that could ever be of use to me."

"I was getting funding from my home, but it seems they are not interested in my dream anymore. This is why I come to you. Thirty percent looks small to you, but believe me, it is more than you think."

Eli Stone lifts the cover on the wooden crate.

"Seems to me this is what you need."

Cesar de Santa looks inside the crate and sees dozens of shrink-wrapped bundles of cash.

"What is this?"

"This? This is your funding. All the money you haven't gotten from home. Did I forget to tell you that we took it? Oh yeah, we took it. See, my spies in Queens told me about your money from 'la Familia' and I decided to take it," Stone sneers.

"You took my money? You took my money! How? When? Do you know what I do to thieves? You have no idea who you are dealing with. I am going to make you pay for this!"

"You shoulda thought about that before you told your men to shoot me."

Stone raises his pistol and shoots de Santa in the head before pushing Vincenzo down behind the crate. Men with guns appear from both sides of the lot. Gunfire erupts and the smell of gunpowder and hot lead fills the air. Men scream in pain as bullets rip through their bodies and their blood paints the ground red. After more than twenty minutes, Stone and his men gain the upper hand and the rest of de Santa's men scatter like rats. De Santa and twenty-one of his men are killed and six of Stone's men lie dead. An untold number of men on both sides are wounded and in need of medical attention.

"It was a bad night to be in Flatbush." Thomas Marcini winces. "The news reporters said there were more than six hundred bullet casings found at the site, and you couldn't walk more than ten feet without walking in blood. As for de Santa's cash, most of it paid our boys' funerals or medical bills. The rest bought us Cesar's businesses in Queens. We bought our competition, but let me tell you, it was a hell of a time telling the rest of de Santa's boys we owned them."

Chapter 6

Thomas Marcini looks through more photographs.

"There he is, smug son of a bitch. Frank Lucas. Thanks to his handiwork in building a heroin pipeline from Harlem to Buffalo, we had the DEA, FBI, XYZ crawling on us day and night. Their thought was that if one organization were pushing the smack, they all were. But Grandad never dealt with that stuff. Guns, cars, nightclubs, money laundering, you always knew what kind of person you were dealing with. Not the same with drugs. Those people are messed up, and my grandfather never wanted to poison our city with that stuff. He always said, 'We give our people life. Heroin is not life.'"

"Your grandfather was a real saint. Let people shoot each other over petty things instead of their next fix. A real saint."

"Call it what you want, detective, but we weren't out there pedaling the trash, poisoning people. We wanted to keep it as easy as possible. No drugs, no problems. The feds though didn't care, they treated us like the scum of the earth. And if it weren't for Lucas, it never woulda happened."

March 1, 1972

With the crackdown on illegal narcotics and organized crime, city law enforcement and government agencies have pooled their resources to identify and halt the operations of more than a dozen crime families in the state of New York alone. A byproduct of this type of cooperation is the birth of the "new neighborhood watch." Adults and children created a network to alert drug dealers and various other criminal activities. With this new development, the FBI has decided to spearhead a new tactic in rooting out the worst offenders.

An FBI car parks in front of the Marcini house, a female agent steps out, walks to the door, and rings the doorbell. Anthony Marcini answers.

"Can I help you, missy?"

"I'm FBI agent Lucy Keller, I need to speak with Mr. Vince Marcini?"

"First, it's Vincenzo, don't make me tell you again. Second, what's your business?

"Right, noted. And your name is?"

"Not your business. Why are you here?"

"I told you, I need to speak with Mr. Marcini."

"He's not here and we're not doing business with the FBI."

"So you are working together, all I needed to know. Thank you." Agent Keller walks away.

Thomas Marcini holds a picture of FBI agent Keller.

"She hounded us for months, trying to put us in the same group with Lucas. She even tried planting bricks of coke in a warehouse we didn't even own, but she never got close to a conviction. Still, we needed to do something fast, so we set her up to look like she was working with Frank Lucas. A few days after we gave the feds evidence that said so, she was fired and then arrested. From what I hear, the feds like their own dealing drugs even less than the real dealers. So, after a quick trial, she was sentenced to six years in medium security."

"So, you shut down a good cop just to keep your hands clean?" Detective Phillips shouts.

"You make it sound worse than it is. I mean, we weren't running the smack, so we had to get the heat off."

"Right, by making a good cop look dirty. Didn't you say you were the good guys?"

"We are, detective. But the feds wouldn't see things our way. They believed if we were selling stolen cars, those cars were full of drugs, and we were going down for it. They wanted to shut down an operation that had too much to lose. I know you don't agree, but if we hadn't done something they would have beaten us on a technicality. You see a good cop suffer; we see a means to an end. That meant we could keep turning the green. Little did we know it would bite us in the ass.

"In the winter of Seventy-Five, Frank Lucas was shut down for good. In turn, that meant the FBI stopped looking into us for drugs because Lucas went down in his own house in Tea-Neck. You imagine getting arrested in your place and the feds relieve you of more than half a million?

"I remember the story; the FBI took him down when they finally had enough evidence to convict. They locked him up and took I believe three million in heroin. That's enough to make a drug dealer cry.

"Well, that's what they wanted to do to us, storm the house take our stuff, and throw us in a box. When it came to our family, they didn't seem to care about probable cause. They only cared about clearing their desks of the 'Marcini crime case' but thanks to Lucas, it never happened."

Chapter 7

Detective Phillips turns over a photograph.

"What about her?"

A blushingly sentimental Thomas Marcini picks up the picture of a beautiful young woman, with long auburn hair, gorgeous green eyes, and ruby red lips. She wears a shimmering yellow sundress and pearl white high heels.

"Ah, man. Mattie Jane Carpenter. Eli Stone's second love. She moved to Brooklyn from Newark in sixty, and was a waitress at Dubrow's. Spring of sixty-one, Eli walked in and sat down for lunch. She took his order and became enthralled by his voice and the way he talked. With that, she kept finding reasons to go back to his table. Stone wouldn't admit it at first, but he liked her the first time they met, too. He made it a habit to have lunch there at least twice a week, and pretty soon they were havin' serious feelings about each other. After three or four months of dating, she moved into his place in Midwood. Though Stone never really told Mattie what he did for a living, she understood that it was usually better not to ask questions. But oh, Lord. They were in love. The first time he brought her by the house, he had just settled a debt with an overworked dock worker who couldn't make ends meet, and he was excited to give my grandpa the good news. As soon as she walked through the door, every neck in that house just about snapped.

"'Benvenuto, Caro. Welcome, darling welcome!' shouted a gleeful Vincenzo Marcini.

"'You are every bit beautiful as Eli has told me. Come please come, we have just put supper on the table. I hope you are hungry!'

"'Thank you, ah, Mr.?'

"'Vincenzo, darling please, call me Vincenzo.'

"'Thank you, Vincenzo. Your house is very beautiful.'

"'Thank you, dear, please sit, sit. We have so much to talk about. Like how you managed to catch the eye of one of my favorite people?'

"'Oh, my, he is just the sweetest. He came into Dubrow's where I work, and I believe in love at first sight. After a few weeks, he asked me out, and I said yes.'

"'What did you do?'

"'Oh, he took me to Nathan's for a hotdog, then we went for a walk through the Botanic Garden. That's kinda been our thing. He is so romantic; I just love it.'

"Eli stone sits down at the table across from Mattie and to Vincenzo's left from the head of the table. Stone hands Vincenzo a sheet of paper and watches him read.

"'Jimmy Winters? From the docks?'

"'Yup, got a promotion, a bonus, and a raise. He called me personally and told me he had his square.'

"'He paid you four thousand dollars right on the spot?'

"'Yup, he was real happy about it. Handed me this envelope and said it's all here. I asked him why he didn't wait for someone to come to him, and he said he wanted to know if the stories were true.'

"'And what did you tell him?' Vincenzo smiles.

"'I just said, don't believe everything you hear.'

"Mattie squirms in her chair, captivated by Eli's story and the way he speaks to his boss.

"'Shoulda seen him light up when he saw me walking up the dock. He looked like a kid that just saw Santa Clause. Apparently, he heard stories of my work and wanted to see it for himself. Never been one to showboat, but I suppose it's not all bad to have an admirer.'

"She was madly in love with him, I tell ya. She told everybody in her family about her boyfriend. The Carpenter family though didn't seem too crazed about Mattie dating someone like Stone, her being tied to our family felt like a slap in the face to them. She didn't care what they thought. He was her whole world. He changed everything for her. December 16, nineteen- seventy-three, they got married in the church my grandpa got married in, and they were off and running.

"I always found it curious how he could go into the city, make sometimes life-altering decisions, and go home like not much took place. But that's the way it was for him. I don't know personally, but I can only guess he had a way of putting a cork on whatever had happened each day, so when he got home, he could just focus on her. She made him better, she made him feel alive, and he did the same for her. So when the call came, and she heard Eli was dead, Mattie damn near fell apart. Sixteen years of marriage, and he was still a soldier at heart. We didn't see much of Mattie after that, but she came around a few days after the funeral. I won't say she knew Eli was still a lion, but I do know she had made peace with his death."

Chapter 8

"By summer of seventy-five, people were already getting ready for the bicentennial, and thanks to the fearmongering on Capitol Hill, people all over the country were afraid of a takeover from one of our enemies, probably Russia. With that fear began the build of urban armies ready to take on any force that came to us. But first, they needed weapons, and man was there money to be made. All we needed to do now was find a supplier. Historically speaking, who has the most guns? You guessed, The military. We made deals with every military station from Massachusetts to North Carolina."

"Wait, you bought guns from the military and sold them to American citizens?" The detective writhes.

"What did you think, the Marines just misplaced two truckloads of M-16s?

"We bought weapons and ammo from every military station that would give us the time of day, and we sold 'em to anybody that wanted to buy. At two-fifty a rifle, we made more money than we ever did on booze. We sold guns to civilian militia from Pennsylvania to South Dakota. We were everywhere, and we were watching the cash roll in. I swear it was the best idea we had since buying the Copa, and half of the Latin nightclubs in Brooklyn.

"That is, until Eli saw a twelve-year-old kid running around with an M-16 playing soldier. It was the only time I ever saw him raise his voice at my grandfather.

"Eli Stone stomps into the Marcini house and kicks Vincenzo's office door off its hinges.

"'Who the hell gave the order to sell rifles in Brooklyn? Somebody answer me now! I just saw James Murphy's youngest boy running in the street with a gun. Not a play gun, a real gun. He doesn't know what the fuck to do with it, and it's only a matter of time before he manages to load it and shoot someone! Now, who gave the damn order?'

"Vincenzo stands up from his desk.

"'Eli, Eli, relax. I didn't know, okay? I didn't know. My brother Gregorio is working that avenue. He is a good businessman, and our liquor is not selling as much right now, so he has time to oversee this. Though I haven't spoken to him about the particulars of his dealings as of late, I will, I promise I will.'

"'If you don't talk to him, I will. And you'll be down to three brothers.'

"'I believe you, Eli. Don't worry.'

"Vincenzo drives his green 1975 Oldsmobile Cutlass to the New York dockyard warehouse where Gregorio, a short, pale man, in his late forties, with bold gray hair, wearing a blue business suit manages his weapons sales.

"'Gregorio, I must talk with you now.'

"'Not now, brother, I have a truck coming in twenty minutes for delivery to St. Louis,' Gregorio snaps.

"'Brother, you can talk to me now or you can talk to ELI, later.'

"Gregorio stands up straight and takes a deep breath to center himself.

"'Let's go to my office.'

"Gregorio closes the office door.

"'What is wrong brother? I haven't seen you this nervous since you told Mama you were leaving for America.'

"'Eli came to the house today. He kicked my office door into splinters and demanded to know who I put in charge of weapons sales. He wanted to know why he hadn't been informed of this avenue of profit.'

"'Why is that his concern? We have no problems here.'

"'Eli was driving through Brooklyn and saw James Murphy's youngest boy in the street with an M-16. Now tell me the truth, Gregorio. Did you sell a rifle to the boy?'

"'OH God, no, I did not! I sold it to his older brother, the tall kid with the goatee and mohawk hair. I had no idea he would let the boy play with it. I am so sorry, brother. Please, I will go take it back.'

"'Good idea, if he gives a gun to a child, he does not respect it enough to keep it. However, I want you to make a show of it. Take three of your men and wait until their father comes home. Do not hurt the boy, but take that rifle. Also do not give him his money back. If he doesn't respect his rifle, he doesn't respect his money.'

"'Okay brother, I'll do that.

"'Right.'

"That night, Gregorio and three men drive to James Murphy's house, they arrive just as he gets home from work. Gregorio approaches James.

"'Excuse me, Mr. Murphy, Can I speak with you a moment?'

"'Suppose, what's this about?'

'Well actually, I need to speak to your oldest boy about a recent business transaction.'

"'Alright, come on they're probably inside.'

"'Thank you, sir.'

"James leads all four men into the house where his sons are in the living room playing a game. Gregorio speaks.

"'You're Robert, right?'

A tall, skinny kid about 19 years old stands up.

"'Yeah, who are you?'

"'That's the wrong question kid. The right question, is why are you here?' Gregorio snarls.

"'Um, okay. Why are you here?'

"'Good boy. I sold you a rifle a month ago, an M-16, remember?'

"'Yeah why, you a cop?'

"Gregorio pushes Robert against the living room wall.

"'NO! I'm just a man who doesn't like seeing a kid running around with a REAL GUN!' Gregorio gestures to the young boy on the floor. 'One of my associates saw your little brother here out on the street with YOUR RIFLE! Now I'm going to count to three, and you're going to explain yourself. 1…2…3…"

"'Okay, okay, yes, I let him play with it! But I didn't tell him to take it outside!'

"James slaps his son.

"'You weren't supposed to give him a rifle in the first place! If you buy a gun, any gun you keep it locked up! Now get your arse down that hall and bring me that gun.'

"'I was just going to say the same thing.'

"Robert walks down the hallway, an M-16 in his hands. His father takes the rifle and hits him with it.

"'Get this gun out of my house. I don't want to see this ever again.'

"'That's why I'm here.'

"'What about my money?'

"'What about your money? If you don't respect a gun, how will you respect money? The answer, is you won't. But you're a tax-paying man, consider it a write-off.'

"Yeah man, gun sales were through the roof," Marcini grins.

"In January of seventy-six, we were selling so many guns that we couldn't keep our warehouse full. Our suppliers from the military told us they needed to take a break because their rifles were disappearing too quickly. So, they put us in contact with their production companies, and we started buying from them. That's how we built the biggest chain of firearm distribution that you never heard of. Boy, oh boy, when we started buying right from the manufacturer, the dollars just stacked faster."

"Must've been hard counting all that cash."

"Not when you have nineteen banks to sift your paper through. Our problems with gun sales didn't come down until Stone found out that street gangs were buying our heat to shoot cops. I don't quite know how to define it, but it's like watching a volcano erupt. He went off the handle, completely insane. Promised to make changes real quick. They say the thunder that came down that day was felt across the state. No one, not even the hardest criminal, would have done what he did. But I'll tell you this, he changed the direction in a frickin' hurry."

Chapter 9

Eli Stone climbs into the cab of a pickup truck headed for a sale in Harlem.

"Hey, man this my truck. This my sale."

"We are not selling guns to these street gangs anymore. Now you get up out this truck before your guts decorate the floor."

The driver looks down at a bowie knife directed at his stomach.

"Hey, man I ain't even supposed to be here today. Fact I'm feeling kinda sick, think I'ma go home."

Stone drives the pickup to the meet site in Morningside Park. He checks his coat and pockets, and then stares at himself in the mirror. As he arrives at the meet site, Stone's stomach churns with anger, contemplating how it has come to this, how did we get to street gangs shooting cops? When he parks, he is greeted by an empty viewing area with a fresh layer of snow. Just then three men walk up the stairs and toward the truck. A young man in a heavy winter coat leans into the open passenger window.

"You ain't the regular guy. The regular guy is some sorta Italian dude."

"He's sick today. You won't see him for a while," Stone whispers.

"Damn, too bad. Gotta stay healthy though, right?"

"Depends on how many bullets you eat."

Stone pulls his pistol, a pristine Colt 1911 .45, and fires two bullets into the buyer's chest, who drops an envelope of cash inside the pickup. Stone rolls out the driver's door and shoots the remaining two men. After he reloads, he kills the second man and stands over the third.

"Killing cops with our guns is bad for your health." Bang.

"He didn't stop there, oh no. He went to every street gang and told them exactly what he did. He told them if they used Marcini's guns against the police, they could expect the same verdict. He said, 'Mercy is given to those who use it.' That was the coldest thing I ever heard him say."

Thomas Marcini picks up a picture of a Police officer in a heavily decorated dress uniform.

"Then there's this man. The true pretender, blue and blue through and through. This guy spent weeks believin' he was the hero the city needed. Right until he was told he wasn't. If only I could have been in that house that night, I heard the Commish threw a tantrum like a toddler hearing the word no."

"Eli Stone drives his car across the Brooklyn Bridge into Manhattan's upper east side. He parks in front of a pearl white townhome near the river.

"Now the police wouldn't admit it, but if it weren't for Stone's work, they would lose a lot of cops. Street gangs and drug dealers were taking shots whenever they had a chance, and if it weren't for Stone, you woulda gone through the academy in about four days. And the cops, they took all the credit for making New York's streets safer. That was until Stone was sent to the police commissioner's house to 'convince' him to pay his due."

Eli Stone approaches the townhome and invites himself inside, finds the dining room, and sits down at the table.

"I'm sure you don't mind if I help myself to some spaghetti right, commissioner Johns?"

Police commissioner Johns, a fourth-generation cop, with chiseled cheekbones, a sharp nose, steel blue eyes, and a perfect complexion looks up from his newspaper.

"Be my guest. Mr.?"

"Right."

"I'm sorry, who are you?"

"That depends on you. I'm your best friend, guardian angel. Or I'm everything you fear. A car bomb, a hit squad, a crazy man in the back seat waiting for you."

"W-What do you want?"

"You have avoided telling the people of New York who is really protecting this city and we're done waiting for our share of the profit."

"I have no idea what you're talking about, my men are out there fighting crime. MY MEN! I don't know you! Who you represent, for all I know you're just a stranger who walked into the wrong house."

"Hmm, I see, so you think the Eighth Avenue Rollers just picked up their flags and left town. Or maybe the Garden Grove Kings just disappeared. I think there are bigger men in play here, commissioner. Rather, I KNOW there are bigger men in play. So, this is what you're gonna do. My spies in the PD tell me that your end of the department receives an eighty-thousand-dollar grant from D.C. every month to support your precincts. You are going to give us fifty percent."

"FIFTY PERCENT!" Commissioner John's scream.

"That's right, fifty percent, a man from our organization will meet you in your office as a spokesman for our agreement. The day after the grant is deposited, you will retrieve forty thousand in cash, in a plain envelope and nothing more. Because you're the commissioner, no one will suspect you're involved with any kind of shady business. Remember, your image protects you."

"I can't just give you forty grand per month! People will begin to wonder why our grant is getting smaller. What about the people in my office? They'll get suspicious. The same man every month leaving with an envelope. You have to think about the consequences."

"Consequences? Sure, let's talk consequences. I'll give you a choice. Agree to the conditions and keep pretending you protect the city. Or tell me to go to hell, and all the protection stops. We work all over this town, you have thirty thousand cops in this city, imagine what'll happen when the bad guys have more guns than the cops."

Chapter 10

Thomas Marcini unfolds an old newspaper. The top headline reads. "Hill-crest Ave Savings Robbed."

"By summer of seventy-six, we had a gun in every hand from Bangor to Miami, and Philly to Milwaukee. And the commissioner, he was doing his part. We had him by the short and curly's, and every time he tried to resist, we reminded him just what we do. You remember that bank on Hillcrest Avenue that lost over three million?"

"Let me guess, you robbed it?" Detective Phillips asked.

"No, we just didn't stop the guys who did. Why? Because it's the bank that controls the PD's payroll. He tried refusing again in October, and then there was the fire at the Puerto Rican Social Club on Morris Avenue. Thirty-three dead, another twenty-five hurt. The Cubans thought the Puerto Ricans were trying to move on their turf. So, we gave 'em a target. After that, the commissioner played ball like a good boy."

"You let a lot of people, innocent people, get hurt so you could keep getting paid!"

"Hey, you don't get into this business for the charm bracelets. You do it for the paper. Money makes the world go 'round, and if you don't have it, you'll do anything to get it.

"The bicentennial came and went without a sound, because like any other news story, it had no weight. But that didn't stop us from being afraid, because that was the year the oil wars got rough. The American people believed that due to low oil stocks and high gas prices, we were going to war with anybody that was gonna cut off our oil lines. OPEC was squeezing as much as they could out of every country they could, but three years later when the Russians got up the nerve to invade Afghanistan, the world's vision quickly moved over to the Middle East. Then when we sent our boys over, people thought we would get invaded, so they bought every gun we had."

"So, you stopped profiting from America's birthday, and you went to profiting from actual death?" Detective Phillips muses. "Interesting, I love how you'll just try to make a buck on anything. No shame, no regard if you should. Just, can we?"

"Listen, detective, you don't understand it, because you're an honest man. That's hard to find these days, but believe me, if you walked in our shoes, you'd see things my way. When you realize how easy it is to make money on necessity, you're gonna want to corner the market.

"In seventy-seven, my sister Victoria turned twenty, and she was destined to be a model. So, she got excited when New York fashion week came around. That meant she'd make herself known to the fashion icons and land a modeling gig with a guy like Valentino. So, she makes her pitch to the head of model talent, and was told, 'drop ten pounds, then call me.'

"I bet she was heartbroken." Detective Phillips sighs. "What a rotten thing to say to someone that wants to work in your industry."

"She was, but not for long. Vicky called Eli at home and told him what happened. Now, Eli always thought of Victoria as his niece, so when he heard what was said to her, he flipped his lid."

Eli Stones Plymouth Fury roars to a stop in front of fashion week. As he gets out, he is met by a weeping Victoria Marcini.

"Eli, I can't believe-"

"Where did you interview?"

"Just inside, they have an office for model applications."

"Show me."

Victoria leads Eli into the building where model interviews are being held. Eli asks for the person in charge and is quickly taken down the hall to meet the head of model talent.

"Whoa, what a specimen. Hello, I'm Sylvia Par-

"Who the hell are you?"

"-ker. Um, sorry?"

"I said, who are you? Are you the one that called my niece fat? Did you actually say, "drop ten pounds, then call me?"

"You seem to be new to the whole modeling thing. See, as an agent to the major designers, I reserve the right to decide who gets hired and who doesn't. Your niece here, while she is pretty, she lacks the body structure that the designers look for. Okay, sure, maybe I was a bit harsh, but I have to keep my customers happy."

"You like your job?"

"Of course."

"You wanna keep doing it?"

"U-um."

"You either give my niece a shot, or I'll give you mine. Here's the thing, you take my shot, I'll be at your funeral tomorrow."

"Welcome aboard, Ms. Marcini, I know you're gonna fit right in," says a visibly shaken Sylvia.

"That's what family means, detective. When you are willing to risk everything to see your people succeed. That was Eli Stone."

"That is a proud story Thomas, I'm glad your sister is doing well for herself. Look, you've told me everything from the beginning, now how does all of it draw up to two weeks ago? I like a good story as much as the next guy, but you need to start putting things together. Did you come here to waste my time? We've been here four hours now, and I have no idea what happened at that courthouse."

"Relax, detective. I'm getting there, there's a lot of details you still need. It ain't easy being the family historian, ya know. Try keeping the history straight after twenty-nine years and a lot of bourbon.

"By nineteen-eighty, we were sitting so well a guy like you could retire yesterday, numbers-wise, we were pulling in about twenty-five grand per day. When the times changed to fit the culture, we changed right with it and there was nothing that could stop us. Right until my great uncle Thomasso, you know, the one grandad put in charge of the nightclubs and money laundering.

"Well, he got to talking to this woman who he thought was a tourist. Well surprise, she wasn't. She was the FBI's newest ploy in undermining our business. We'd been dodging them for years now, and we figured 'em out every time they tried to sneak back in. But whoa, talk about unforeseen. I mean, they took a lady agent, a beautiful woman, and sent her to find a way into our lives. Now great uncle Thomasso, he's a smart man, but because he ran the nightclubs, he was also a pure Italian ladies' man.

"And that slicked-back hair and million-dollar smile worked every time. That meant he went out front every night and got the ladies all riled up with his charm and persona, and then he made sure they all had a good time.

"So, when he brought special agent blondie into the fold, he changed. Once he got bit by the love bug, he let her in on every sit-down and she had one of them listening devices on her every time. The FBI recorded years of deals, business meetings, cash transactions, and everything else. Then they put it all together and finally made it stick."

Chapter 11

Vincenzo Marcini sits at his desk discussing the matter of the FBI with his brothers Gregorio, Anthony, Thomasso, And Ignacio, a thin, pale man well into his fifties with thinning gray hair, a proud bushy mustache, and skin that time has not been kind to. Eli Stone sits in a chair staring at the floor, listening as Vincenzo curses out his brother.

"Damn you, Thomasso, how can you be so stupid! Why did you not have her checked out when you had the chance? You could have found out who she was BEFORE WE GOT INTO THIS MESS! We have people just for this. You had a responsibility to this family to see that we have no law enforcement problems. YOU FAILED!"

"I'm, sorry brother, I didn't think she was going to bring us this trouble. I believed she was just another woman; she never gave me a reason to investigate. I saw no need to waste time trying to find out her whole life."

"They are bringing down charges of money laundering, embezzlement, and business fraud. AND YOU LET THEM DO IT! Because you think with your testicloi instead of your brain! I put you in charge of the nightclubs because you know how to network, build security, and quietly bring in money. But no! You prefer to smile at women and lay with the ones who look at you twice. They sent a Lupo! A wolf dressed as a woman, and you let her fall in your arms!"

Thomas Marcini picks up a picture of a New York federal judge.

"By the end of summer eighty-nine, the FBI had torn our lives to pieces. Commissioner Johns was arrested for his involvement with us, heads of military affairs were called down because of our business dealings, and every person that we dealt with or had on paper over thirty-eight years was either arrested or subpoenaed for their involvement with us. It was like a hurricane of paperwork, everywhere we looked there was another person we dealt with on tv in cuffs, the news anchor griping about how could we have stretched so far. "That brings us to two weeks ago. My grandfather called a meeting with everyone who had a stake in the fold and wanted to know how to salvage the business. Now we knew Eli was loyal to my grandfather, but we didn't know just how deep that loyalty ran. I mean, it wasn't like he owed his life, but it's exactly what he gave."

"I want to know where we stand on moving or selling our remaining merchandise, we need to make sure our hands are clean of as much as we can. The last thing we need now is loose ends we don't know about. So, tell me what you know."

"Gregorio and I have just sold the last weapons and cars we have in warehouses. They are being scrubbed as we speak. As soon as the boys finish, they are getting on a bus out of town."

"Good work, Ignacio, What about you, Anthony? I know you had to pick up a lot of slack when Thomasso was arrested. How are things going for you?"

"The feds are all over the night clubs so we can't go anywhere near. But as far as collections, everything is clean. They can't track anything to us, period. The nightclubs we can't do anything about."

"I understand," Vincenzo breathes. Thank you for cleaning up your end. "Eli, what do you think we should do?"

Everyone in the room turns to look at Eli. He looks up from the floor, stands up, looks at Vincenzo, and leaves.

"The next day we hear about a massive gunfight at the courthouse on the news. He must've thought that by taking out the judge, it meant he would take the weight and we might walk. Tough work, making life-altering decisions, I suppose. Tough work. But I mean, what a story though, right? One man takes on a dozen FBI agents and even more cops, and he succeeds? Though, not quite the way we wanted.

Eli stone parks his car in front of the courthouse. He looks inside his jacket, checks his pockets, and exits the car. As he approaches the front doors, he smiles at the police officers in front of the building. Once he enters, he sees Judge Peter Moreno, a second-generation Latin-born judge. And the judge presiding over the Marcini Crime case. He is walking with three FBI agents as they discuss his safety during the trial.

"HEY JUDGE!"

The judge turns around just in time to see Stone raise his pistol and fire. The ensuing gunfight lasts almost forty minutes. In the battle eight agents are killed, four are injured as are three courthouse police officers.

"In a remarkable twist of fate, agent Lucy Keller, the one we set up with Lucas? She's the one who shot Stone at the courthouse. His adrenaline was pumping so hard, it took eight bullets to finally put him down. And when he did go down, he went out smiling. I think there was a part of him that always longed for the fight. He was a gentleman, always kind and caring. But when you stepped over the line or broke his moral code, he made you regret it. You may not agree, detective, but his decisions made sure we all keep breathing. Whether that's in a cell, or on the road to anywhere, I'm gonna miss that man a whole lot."

The detective lays down a newspaper dated Sept .30, 1989. The top headline reads, "Marcini Crime Family, Finally Brought to Justice."

"So, after all that," the detective puzzles, "almost forty years in operation, it comes down to a man who wanted to save his bosses can, but could only think of one way to do it?"

The tape recorder clicks off.

"What do you want me to say, detective? Once a soldier, always a soldier? He had one job. Protect the business. He did that the only way he knew how. Brute force.

"This life ain't for the faint of heart. But when you love something and want to protect it, you have to give it all you got. Sometimes you win, sometimes you lose. And sometimes, you get to go out the way you planned it."

THE END.